TALES

FOR

THE

SEVENTH

DAY

Tales for the Seventh Day

A Collection of Sabbath Stories

BY

Nina Jaffe

ARTWORK BY

Kelly Stribling Sutherland

SCHOLASTIC PRESS

NEW YORK

Library of Congress Cataloging-in-Publication Data Available.
Library of Congress catalog card number: 99-056979

ISBN 0-590-12054-9

10 9 8 7 6 5 4 3 2 1   0/0 01 02 03 04

Printed in the United States of America   37
First edition, September 2000

The display type was set in Cirrus and Garamond 3.
The text type was set in 13-point Garamond 3.
Book design by Marijka Kostiw

FOR MY BROTHER, DAVID;

HIS WIFE, VICTORIA;

AND THEIR SON,

MY BEAUTIFUL

NEPHEW JACOB

HERMAN.

— N.J.

ACKNOWLEDGMENTS

THE AUTHOR IS GRATEFUL TO MARK STEIN — BANK STREET GRADUATE, JUDAICA SPECIALIST AND TEACHER WHO PROVIDED INVALUABLE ASSISTANCE WITH RITUAL DETAILS, BACKGROUND RESEARCH, AND REVIEW OF THE STORIES. MANY THANKS ALSO TO NORA GAINES AT THE BANK STREET COLLEGE LIBRARY; THE ELDGRIDGE STREET SYNAGOGUE RESTORATION PROJECT STAFF; THE JEWISH THEOLOGICAL SEMINARY LIBRARY; AND RABBI MICHAEL STRASSFELD OF ANSCHE CHESED SYNAGOGUE IN NEW YORK CITY, FOR HIS TEACHING, VISION, AND INSPIRING EXAMPLE.

— N . J .

Table
of
Contents

List
of
Illustrations

TALES
FOR
THE
SEVENTH
DAY

Introduction

EVERY FRIDAY NIGHT, many Jewish families from all over the world share in rituals that have been in existence for centuries, ushering in a holy day that lasts until sundown the following evening. Candles are lit, prayers and blessings are chanted, and people gather to enjoy a festive meal to honor and celebrate Shabbat — the day on which, according to the Hebrew Bible, God rested after the work of Creation. In North America, there are many different ways to worship in the Jewish faith. Some people

1

follow each law very strictly. Others have changed or adapted the observances according to their beliefs and values. Still, many Jews know or recognize the importance of celebrating Shabbat — the holiest day of the Jewish week.

Traditionally, it is the mother of the house who gathers the family together as she lights two candles and repeats the ancient blessing, "Blessed be You, O Lord, Creator of the Universe, who has sanctified us and commanded us to light the Sabbath candles." Children join in to sing "Shalom Aleichem," a song that welcomes the Sabbath angels into their home. In some homes, parents will place their hands over the heads of their children and say a prayer, "May the Lord bless you and keep you, may the Lord shine his countenance upon you and grant you peace." Then a special cup of wine, the kiddush cup, is raised. The family says a prayer to bless the seventh day and thank God for the creation of the world and the gift of Shabbat. One of the children will take the cover off of the challah loaves — bread that has been twisted in braids — and repeat the blessing over it: "Blessed be You, O Lord, Creator of the Universe, who brings forth bread from the earth." Then, and only then, will the family sit down to share the meal. Sometimes, at the end of the meal, someone will start to hum a special song called a *zemer* — a Sabbath melody — to extend the joy and spirit of this age-old day of rest.

Celebrating the seventh day — Shabbat — is embedded in Jewish law, custom, and belief, going back to the divine commandment, "You shall honor the seventh day and make it holy." In many communities, families attend synagogue services, where every Sabbath a new portion or chapter of the Torah is chanted. Study and quiet reading are all associated with traditional activities of the day. In the late afternoon, a meal called *seudah shlishit,* "the third meal," is eaten, and at sundown on Saturday evening the family performs the *havdalah* ceremony — the closing ceremony — that has its own special blessings and ritual. At the close of the Sabbath it is customary to wish your friends *"Shavua tov"* which means "have a good week."

According to the Jewish tradition, the purpose of the Sabbath is to recall, honor, and celebrate God as the ultimate source of the creation of the universe and of all life. Throughout the centuries, rabbis and scholars developed many laws — called *halachah* — to protect the Sabbath. These great sages classified certain activities — called *melachot* — as contradicting the Torah's commandment: "Thou shalt do no work." These included plowing, reaping, writing, and sewing. In our times, these laws have been adapted to take modern technology into account. For example, in very observant communities, it is forbidden on the Sabbath to turn electricity on or off, in respect for the halachic prohibition against lighting fires. Not every family will follow these laws exactly, but they form part of the background of many Sabbath customs and traditions.

Unlike other holidays that occur once a year, Shabbat is woven into the rhythm of each week. The great Jewish scholar and philosopher, Abraham Joshua Heschel, (1907–1972), wrote about the Sabbath as "a palace in time." Because Jews in the Diaspora were often moving from one region to another, keeping the holidays and especially the Sabbath rituals helped create a sense of continuity and a common spiritual heritage. The idea of sacred time helped Jews keep their identity — no matter what country or region of the world they were living in, no matter how near or far they lived from Jerusalem, the holy city; no matter if they lived in small country villages or bustling cities. In our world of television, computers, and global travel, keeping the Sabbath is still a part of observant Jewish life — from Jerusalem to New York, from London to Buenos Aires.

Whether or not a family or community observes all of the many customs associated with the day, Shabbat continues to be a time for gatherings, special events, and prayers in Jewish communities throughout the world. In rabbinic literature, or *Midrash,* legends say that the Sabbath, along with the Torah and the day of *Yom Kippur,* was in existence before the creation of the world. Adam and Eve were blessed with the light of Shabbat in the Garden of Eden. A legendary river, the Sambatyon, flows all week, except on Shabbat. In the *Kabbalistic* or mystical tradition, the Sabbath took on the image of a bride or queen.

4

In the sixteenth century, the mystics of *Safed* greeted the Sabbath at sunset with singing and dancing, dressed in white robes, as if to greet a bride. Their poetry became part of contemporary Sabbath liturgy, as in the song *"L'chah Dodi* — Come my beloved, let us greet the bride, let us greet the Sabbath Queen." There is also a belief in the mystical tradition that on the Sabbath, everyone receives the divine gift of a second soul — a "Sabbath soul." The Sabbath gives a taste, say the legends, of a time when justice, sustenance, and peace will fill the world — not just one day a week, but every day. In some communities in North America, the Middle East, Europe, and Israel, it is a custom for all stores, businesses, and schools to be closed from early Friday afternoon to the following evening. A deep sense of quiet, calm, and tranquility descends upon the streets and homes for these precious hours.

The stories in this book are drawn from the wealth of Jewish lore and legend: from the Talmud — books of Jewish law and custom — to folktales and the oral tradition. We hope that as you read these tales, you will be drawn into the world of magic, harmony, mystery, and peace, that is part of the spirit and ritual of the Sabbath day.

His cloak was covered with feathers of all colors . . .

The
Most
Important
Day

LONG AGO, AFTER the creation of the world, the days of the week got into an argument. Each one said that it was the most important. The first day was dressed in a swirl of black and silver. One half of his face was dark as soot, the other was pale as the moon. He spoke in a deep voice, "I am the most important day, because it was on my day that God separated light from darkness. Without me, the world would be in total chaos. There would be no evening and no morning. I am the most important day!"

The second day took his turn. Above his head there was a shining cloud, and around his feet ran streams of rushing water. "My brother, you are wrong. It was on my day that the Holy One created the firmament of the heavens, separating the waters above from the waters below. Without my day, there would have been no place to build the earth! I am the most important day." And the waters gurgled and bubbled around him.

Now the third day stood up. His shoulders were covered with sand and soil. Twigs and branches stuck out of his pockets, and a garland of flowers circled his head. "There is no argument here! It was on my day that God created the earth itself, with all of its green plants, flowers, and trees. Without my day, there would be no land! The earth would be barren and bare! I am the most important day!" And flower petals fell from his head.

The sun began to turn in the sky as the fourth day stepped forward. His cloak was covered with moons, planets, and stars. Twinkling lights sparkled around him as he raised his hands to speak. "The discussion ends here! How could any of you think of your own significance! It was on my day that God placed the sun, the moon, and stars in the sky to mark the seasons and the passing of years. Without my day, the sky would be black and empty. There would be no time, no change — all would be still! I am the most important day!"

The fifth day rushed forward. His cloak was covered

with feathers of all colors. His sleeves were lined with silvery scales. "Come my brothers, let us not quibble this way! It was on my day that God created the creatures that inhabit the sea and the sky — from the hawk to the sparrow; from the smallest minnow to great Leviathan. It was on my day that the earth was filled with living creatures! Look at me and you'll know who is most important!"

Now the sixth day stood up — and he was taller than all the rest. His voice was deep and rough. He was covered with paw prints of many animals, and on his vest, the marks of a human hand. "There is no day more important than mine, because on my day God created the beasts of the field, from the mighty tiger to the little mouse. But most important, it was on the afternoon of my day that the Holy One made the first man and woman — human beings created in God's own image. Which of you could be more important than that?"

And so the days continued to argue back and forth, their voices growing louder and louder as clouds swirled, waters rushed, leaves and branches flew in every direction. The seventh day sat by herself, alone and quiet, dressed in a simple white gown. Finally, they all turned to her and said, "What do you have to say for yourself? Why do you sit there in silence?"

She looked up at them and replied, "My brothers, each of you is important, for without any of you the world would be lacking and incomplete. There would be no skies, no earth, no stars, no people. But it is through me that God gave to the world and its creatures the greatest gift of all."

"What do you mean?" they shouted, in one voice.

The seventh day smiled when she spoke. As the sun set and darkness filled the sky, she held out her hands. A glowing flame appeared before them as she drew the days of the week into a circle and began to sing. "Bless the seventh day and keep it holy. For it was on my day that the world received the gift of peace and rest, *shalom v'minucha*. It was on my day that the world received Shabbat."

. . . he saw a family just sitting down to a meal.

Sabbath
Spice

LONG AGO, WHEN the Jewish people were first scattered to the far corners of the globe, there were many who came to reside in the great kingdom of Persia. There, they lived according to their laws — for even without the Great Temple of Jerusalem, the people could pray to God, celebrate the festive days, and study the holy books. Many had fled the kingdoms of Babylonia and Egypt, to escape war and poverty. They were craftsmen and scholars, nobles and merchants. Among them was a scholar named

Nehemiah. Although his knowledge was great, he lived simply, in a small, stone house with his wife and children. He spent his days teaching and studying. Sometimes he did not see his family until dawn broke in the sky. But every Friday night, at sundown, he was sure to be home to light the candles and usher in the Sabbath with prayers and blessings.

At that time, Persia was ruled by the emperor Cyrus. His armies numbered in the tens of thousands. His laws and power reached from the shores of the Mediterranean to the desert sands of the Indus Valley. Although Cyrus ruled as wisely as he could, he knew that his kingdom was large and there were many people and customs that were unknown to him. One year, he decided to go on a journey, to travel among the towns and provinces so that he could come to know the ways of his subjects. On each stop of his caravan, the local people — be they Medians, Egyptians, or Mesopotamians — treated him with a royal welcome. They brought before him their finest foods, their best musicians, and their wisest priests and scholars.

Toward the end of his journey, he stopped for the night near a small village before returning to Susa, the royal city. The road had been long, and the emperor was hungry and tired. He longed for the comforts of his palace. As the sun set, the night called to him and he wandered out among the village's humble dwellings. Passing a narrow street, he heard a song emanating from one of the houses. Peering into the entranceway, he saw a family just sitting down to a meal. A delicious fragrance reached him and he was drawn to look closer. The head of the house, Nehemiah the scholar, welcomed him in the tradition of hospitality to strangers and invited the traveler to join in the Sabbath meal.

The emperor sat and watched as Nehemiah's wife closed her eyes and said the blessing over the candles. The scholar chanted blessings over the wine and bread, and passed them around for his children and guest to taste. Each course was more delicious than the last. In all of his travels through his provinces, sampling the best that each region had to offer, Cyrus had never tasted such delicious food. Before he left Nehemiah's house, Cyrus begged for the recipe. He wanted to know each of the ingredients so that his own royal cooks could prepare such a feast for him.

Cyrus returned home and commanded his palace cooks to appear before him. "Here is a recipe for a meal. Begin to prepare it at once so that I can call all my friends to enjoy a feast and celebrate my homecoming!"

The cooks went right to work. They found the choicest fish and the finest grains of wheat. They went to the marketplace and bought baskets of sweet dates from the desert oases, and the most aromatic spices, brought all the way from the Indus Valley. When the feast was ready, Cyrus invited his friends. They came and sat around the table, waiting expectantly for their food. Cyrus was the first to touch his plate. But at the first bite, he scowled and threw his goblet to the ground. He was mortified to serve such a meal to his royal friends, after all he had told them of its bounty and flavor.

"Bring in the chief cook! I will have his head! This food tastes nothing like the meal I had at the house of Nehemiah the scholar!" The cook appeared before his master, shivering, despite the warm breezes of desert air that blew through the banquet hall. "Your Royal Highness, I did just as you commanded. I followed the recipe exactly as it was given to me. I can't understand what happened." But the emperor was not satisfied. He began to lift his hand to call for the soldiers to take the cook to prison. The man was terrified. He knew that once Cyrus issued such a command, it would be just a matter of time till the day of his execution. The cook took a chance and spoke in a trembling voice, "Your Royal Highness, before you send me to the gallows, why don't you call on the man who first served you this meal? Maybe he can tell you what is missing here?"

The emperor was now determined to bring the matter to justice, and he sent for Nehemiah to appear before him. When Nehemiah walked in, Cyrus waved a plate before his nose. "When I visited your house, you gave me a recipe for the meal that I enjoyed. But now I have prepared this same meal for all of my guests, and it doesn't taste anything like yours. Don't you know that there is a great punishment for deceiving your emperor, the ruler of Persia?"

Nehemiah inspected the food carefully — each plate and each clay pot in the kitchen. Then he returned before Cyrus and said, "It is true, you have all of the same ingredients. Every spice is there except one, but this one can't be found in any garden or market in your whole kingdom. The sweetness of the meal that you remember is the secret spice — the spice of the Sabbath day — and only those who keep it holy can truly taste its flavor."

As the emperor recalled the meal, for a moment he relived the delights of that Sabbath night — the soft light of the candles, the voices of the children as they prayed and sang, the smiling faces around the table as they shared the bread and wine. Suddenly, he understood what the scholar was talking about. He waved his cook back to the kitchen and invited his guests to complete the meal that was set before them. Nehemiah took his leave, saying, "The emperor is welcome any time to come to our house on a Friday evening to sample our special repast."

From then on, the Jews of Persia enjoyed many years of freedom, peace, and tolerance, all because Cyrus — the royal emperor — had tasted Sabbath spice.

From the shadows he watched the tiny creature . . .

King
David
and the
Spider

DAVID WAS ONE of the greatest kings of Israel. Long before he became king, however, he was a shepherd boy. The prophet Samuel annointed him with a special blessing, for it had been foretold that this young boy, son of Jesse the farmer, would one day rule over all the people of Israel. But in those days, the reigning king was Saul. He was a great warrior who helped to protect his people from the invading Philistines, as well as other enemies. He could also be very jealous and unreasoning. Sometimes he flew into violent rages that lasted for days, and nobody could placate him.

David was also known for his skills as a singer and player of the lyre and harp. His father brought him before King Saul's court to see if he could serve as court musician. Only David's soothing melodies on the harp could calm the rages of King Saul.

David was also very brave. As a small boy he had confronted a fearful lion, and slew it to protect his father's flock. In the time of the war with the Philistines, David was the only one of Saul's soldiers who dared to face the giant warrior Goliath. With taunting words, and armed only with a sling, David let fly a small stone and felled the giant forever. Only then could King Saul's soldiers overcome the invading army. Throughout the land, people sang Saul's praises, but even louder were their praises for David, warrior and court musician, David, son of Jesse.

So it was that David became known to the people, although he was but a servant in King Saul's court. Despite all that he had done for Saul, the jealous king could feel nothing but hatred for the young man, and plotted to banish, or even kill him.

One Sabbath afternoon, David was sitting in a garden. He knew that there was danger around him, but he did not want to believe that he could come to harm in the palace of the king. As he sat, letting his mind roam to more pleasant topics, he caught sight of a small spider, weaving a web between the branches of an olive tree. David had been raised in the faith of his people. He believed in God and honored the commandments, including the observance of the holy day of rest. But as he looked at the spider, a question came to his mind, and in his musings he spoke to God and said, "Oh, Holy One, you have created the world and chosen the people of Israel to observe your commandments. We have a role to play in your world, but what about this spider? Here it works away on the Sabbath, spinning a web that nobody can use. It cannot be worn, it cannot be traded, or shade us from heat or prevent the cold. What is the point of this creature's existence?"

No answer came to David, but still he mused.

Just then, he heard a whistle by the wall. It was Jonathan, son of King Saul. Despite his father's jealousy, the young prince and David had sworn to remain friends. "Quick," said Jonathan, "you must flee at once. My father has sent his soldiers to come and get you. Your life is now truly in danger." Without waiting an instant, David pulled his tunic over his shoulders and rushed out the garden gate. Following a rocky path, he sped away to find a place to hide. From his days as a shepherd, he knew every stone and every corner of every field. But the soldiers were close on his trail.

As evening fell, David found his way to the hills of Judea. There, he heard the baying of dogs and the clattering footsteps of the guards as they ran in swift pursuit. With no place else to hide, he remembered a cave near a spot where he had played as a child. He ran to the cave and wriggled in through the small opening that still remained. He crouched at the back of the cave, shivering with cold and fear. Now he was at a dead end. The soldiers were coming closer and, if they found him, he would have no way to escape.

The baying of the dogs grew louder, and the sound of trumpets clamored over the hillsides. Young David thought that all was lost. There was nowhere else to hide — no tunnel or footpath to escape the shining swords and barbed arrows of King Saul's guard. Just then, a small spider appeared at the mouth of the cave. With lightning speed, she began to weave her web. The silvery lines criss-crossed until a net of silken thread glistening in the moon-light began to stretch across the mouth of the cave. David sat in his hiding place, trying to keep his heart still, his breath from being heard. From the shadows, he watched the tiny creature as she diligently wound her spider silk back and forth, over and under, to complete her work.

The soldiers came running, following the trail that their dogs had found. The rising moon illuminated the mouth of the cave as the dogs barked and growled, pulling and straining at their leather straps. The soldiers ran up, their shields clanking against the stones — but when they reached the opening to the cave, they stopped. One soldier prepared to enter but his companion pulled him back, and shouted, "Are you blind? This cave is covered with a spider's web. It's completely whole and unbroken. Look — you can see it clearly in the moonlight. Nobody has entered this cave for days. That shepherd boy must have gone higher up the hillside. The dogs have picked up a false trail."

David began to breathe again as the soldiers' voices and the baying of their dogs faded into the night. After several hours, he carefully untangled the web and made his way across the mountainsides to shelter.

Years later, the young shepherd boy did become king, as the prophet Samuel had foretold. He was honored and revered by his people for his strength and wisdom. David continued to play and compose music to honor the God of Israel and His holy commandments. Every Friday night, in the palace of Jerusalem, he would light the oil lamps and, in the presence of the priests and his servants, would bless the Holy One for creating the world, and for the seventh day of rest. And as he chanted the blessings, while holding up a goblet of wine, he would say a silent prayer thanking God for the day on which the Holy One created all of the creatures that creep, crawl, swim, or fly over the earth, knowing that even the most humble — even a small gray spider — has a special role, and its own destiny to fulfill.

What could she do with this foolish boy?...

Mottke's
Chicken

ONCE, IN THE town of Vitebsk near the border of Russia and Lithuania, there lived a boy named Mottke. Sometimes his parents would call him Mottkele. He was the kind of child who, if you told him to go upstairs, he would go down. If you asked him to get ready for bed, he would put on his school clothes. And when it was time to milk the cows, he would head out to the chicken coop.

Although his parents loved him, they sometimes were driven to distraction by his ways, but in the end they would shake their heads and say, "Mottke will always be Mottke." His father was a tradesman who often had to travel to make a living for his family. Wherever he was, he always found a way to return home in time to observe the Sabbath with his wife and son. Mottke's mother spent long days working in the town market, selling vegetables that she grew in their small garden. But every Friday afternoon, she left the market early in time to prepare for the day of rest.

On these days, Mottke would always say, "Mother, let me help!" And she did. But because he was Mottke, she gave him chores inside the house, where she could tell him exactly what to do. "Here, Mottke," she would say, "take this broom and sweep out all of the dust." Or she would tell him, "Here, Mottke, take this bucket of water and wash off the table." She never sent him on an errand that would take him far from home, because she never knew what kind of trouble he would get into.

One Friday, however, in the early afternoon, she realized that in her haste to get home from the market, she had forgotten to buy a chicken to cook for dinner. With no other choice, she decided to send Mottke to the market. "Now, Mottkele, take this coin and go straight to the market to find a chicken — a nice fat one that we can have for dinner. Remember, be home by sunset."

Mottke took the coin, put it in his pocket, and set out

across town to the market, whistling as he walked. His mother watched as he went down the road. Then she went into the house to finish her preparations. While she worked, the sun rose in the sky, then began to lower and send its last rays over the horizon. Still, her son hadn't returned. "Where can that Mottkele be?" she asked herself, and ran outside to wait for him by the roadside.

Finally, she saw the boy approaching. He was still whistling, and in his hand, he was carrying a glass of water. "Mottke, where have you been all this time? And where is the chicken? It is almost time for your father to return!"

Mottke looked up. "But, mother, listen to what happened! I went to the market, just like you said, and found the butcher. I told him that I needed a nice, fat, fresh chicken. The butcher held up the chicken, and said, 'Mottke, this is no ordinary chicken. Look at it — so plump and firm! Why this is more than a chicken — it is already like the sweetest chicken fat!'

"So then I knew that chicken fat was *better* than a chicken. I went to the grocer, and asked him for a big jar of his best chicken fat. The grocer held up the jar and said, 'Son, this is no ordinary chicken fat. Look how it gleams and glistens in the jar. It is like golden oil.'

"So then I knew that oil is even *better* than chicken fat. I went to the oil merchant, and asked him for a jar of oil.

He held up a jar of oil, and said, 'Mottke, look at this jar of oil. It is no ordinary oil — it is brought to Vitebsk from the Holy Land itself. It is like the purest spring water.' So then I knew that water was even *better* than oil — it must be the best of all. I went to the well and tossed in the coin you gave me. Then I found a glass, filled it up, and here I am. Now we can have the perfect Sabbath meal."

Mottke's mother shook her head for a moment. What could she do with this foolish boy? Then she remembered that it was, after all, the Sabbath. If she gave him a hiding, it would only break the Sabbath peace. Besides, maybe next week, he would do better. So she picked up the glass of water, gave her son a kiss on the forehead, and took him in the house to celebrate the Sabbath, even without a chicken.

Holding a candle and carrying a staff . . .

A
Riddle
and a
Kiss

ONCE UPON A time, in the city of Seville, Spain, there was a gardener who had three lovely daughters. Their names were Alicia, Esther, and Rina. Every day, they cared for the plants that lined the path to their house. The garden had a lemon tree, roses, almond trees, and all manner of herbs. The most fragrant herb of all was the basil plant. Each day, the girls took their turn weeding, turning the soil, and watering the roots of the precious plant.

Now at that time, the son of a renowned family, Don

Isaaco by name, was living in Seville. In later years, he would acquire his father's estate and noble title. But now he spent his time hunting, fishing, and amusing himself as young nobles did. Don Isaaco was very fond of riddles. He was quite clever, and loved to test people by asking them questions that they could never hope to answer. He considered himself to be far superior in wit and worldly knowledge to any of the inhabitants of Seville.

One day, he went for a walk through the streets and plazas and, coming to the outskirts of the city, he was drawn by the lovely scent of almond branches and lemon trees. It was the home of the gardener. As he came closer he saw Alicia, the eldest daughter, as she bent over the soil, tending to the basil plant. He drew near, and when she looked up, he thought of a riddle:

> *"Young maiden who tends to the garden walk,*
> *How many leaves on the basil plant's stalk?"*

Alicia was startled. As soon as she saw the young noble and heard his words, she blushed and ran into the house, for she had no way of answering him. Whistling to himself, he walked away. He had outwitted another lowly citizen.

The next day he returned and found Esther, the second daughter, tending the garden. He thought to himself, "I'll try my riddle on this one." When she heard his words,

Esther also blushed and ran into her father's house. The young noble felt pleased with his own cleverness.

The next day, he once again returned to the garden. He was beginning to enjoy himself immensely. This time, Rina, the youngest daughter, was tending the flowers and herbs. He leaned over the gate and, as she worked, he repeated his question:

> *"Young maiden who tends to the garden walk,*
> *How many leaves on the basil plant's stalk?"*

But Rina was not taken aback. She stood up and looked at the young man, with his velvet cloak and leather boots, and without a pause, she replied:

> *"I'll give your answer if first you reply,*
> *How many stars fill the night sky?"*

For the first time in his life, the young man was flustered. Someone had dared to answer him back. Since he had no answer for her, he turned on his heels and went back to his castle to plot his revenge.

The next day was Friday. Early in the morning, Don Isaaco threw a cloak over his head, and picked out the finest fish in the kitchen. He wrapped it in cloth and put it in a basket. Then he made his way back to the gardener's house. Once again, Rina was in the garden. He stopped by and called out in the voice of a street peddler, "Fresh fish for the Sabbath. Come buy a tasty morsel from the sea for your Sabbath table." Rina walked to the gate. She didn't recognize the noble youth, but she thought it would be nice to have such a fine fish for Shabbat. "How much for the fish?" she asked. "I'll run to the house and pay you gladly, for in our house it is a joy to celebrate the Sabbath with a festive meal."

Don Isaaco spoke in a disguised voice and said, "Since this is no ordinary fish, no ordinary coin will do. If you want this fish for your Sabbath meal, you must pay me not with coins, but with kisses."

Rina stepped back in shock. Then she thought about what a lovely meal she could prepare for her family and, looking around to make sure that nobody else was there, she said, "Very well," and offered him her cheek.

The noble kissed her enough times for her to be worthy of such a fine Sabbath gift. Rina grabbed her prize and ran into the house. Don Isaaco walked away, chuckling to himself. Some days later, in his own attire, he returned to the garden to find Rina. Once again, he called out his favorite taunt:

> *"Young maiden who tends to the garden walk,*
> *How many leaves on the basil plant's stalk?"*

Without batting an eye, she replied:

"I'll give you your answer if first you reply,
How many stars fill the night sky?"

But now Don Isaaco boldly replied in his peddler's voice:

"I will answer, but tell me first if you wish,
How many kisses did you give me for a Sabbath fish?"

Rina was truly mortified at his words. She realized that it was he who had tricked her and disguised himself as the peddler. This young noble had mocked her honor. She ran into the house and sobbed while Don Isaaco went back to his palace, his sense of dignity restored.

For many days Rina could not be comforted. Her sisters brought her treats. Her father brought her books. But nothing could ease her spirits. In the end, however, she would not let herself be outwitted. She dried her tears and came up with a plan. First, she borrowed a mule from a neighbor's stable. Then she sewed pieces of black cloth together — enough to wrap herself completely — and covered her face with its hood. When all her preparations were complete, she waited until the middle of the night, and then stole her way through secret paths to the castle of young Don Isaaco and his family. She left her mule tied up by the garden wall and quietly found her way into the young man's sleeping chamber.

Holding a candle and carrying a staff, she knocked three times on the floor. Don Isaaco awoke with a start, and saw before him a menacing figure, draped in shadows. "I am the angel of death," said the figure. "Your days on earth are over. Now you must come with me."

The young noble was terrified. "But I am still a young man," he said. "Surely it is not my time to depart the world."

The shrouded figure spoke again. "There is one way for some mortals to extend their life, but only if you are brave."

"I'll do anything," said the youth.

"If you wish to live, you must come out to the garden secretly where nobody can see you."

The noble followed her down the staircase and outside. As soon as they reached the garden wall, Rina said in a hoarse whisper, "If you wish to live you must show your humility by kissing this beast on the nose — one time for each year you wish to live."

The prideful youth was even more horrified. He — the noble Don Isaaco, son of the great family of Seville — kiss a mule? But since it was in the dark of night, he bent down and planted a kiss on the animal's nose. He did so many times, in order to have a long, long life.

"Now be off," said Rina, and waved her staff.

The youth returned to his room and fell into a deep, peaceful sleep.

The next day, feeling in a lively mood, he decided to pay one last visit to the house of the gardener. He called his servants to come along, so that he could show off by challenging the maiden with the rhyme that he knew she would not be able to answer. When he arrived with his retinue trailing behind, there was Rina, modestly sprinkling the garden with water. He knocked on the gate and began to speak:

> *"Young maiden who tends to the garden walk,*
> *How many leaves on the basil plant's stalk?"*

Without hesitating, she replied:

> *"I'll give you your answer if first you reply,*
> *How many stars fill the night sky?"*

The noble was ready. He said:

> *"I will answer, but tell me first if you wish,*
> *How many kisses did you give me for a Sabbath fish?"*

He looked around, gloating. His courtiers nodded in approval. But this time Rina did not run away. Instead, she looked at the noble and spoke in the voice that she had used in her disguise:

"True, I paid for fish with kisses like a fool,
But how many times at midnight did you kiss a mu . . ."

Before she could finish her riddle, however, Don Isaaco threw his sword on the ground with a crash. "Very well," he replied quietly, "you have won the game. I have finally met my match. There *is* someone in the city of Seville as clever as I."

The courtiers looked on in astonishment. How could he speak so respectfully to a mere gardener's daughter? But Rina and Don Isaaco understood each other very well. He did not want anyone to ever hear the last word of her rhyme, or discover how she had tricked him. And she for her part was satisfied, her revenge was complete. Now she could look the young noble in the eye without shame.

The courtiers dispersed, still puzzling over what had occurred. But the young noble realized that he would never meet a maiden as intriguing as Rina. Some days later, he appeared at the garden again, not with a riddle, but with a proposal of marriage. And so it was that Rina, the youngest daughter of the gardener of Seville, married into the noble family of Don Isaaco. They lived happily together for many years, often telling stories and riddles to each other, and to their children. And even today, their descendants say this rhyme, a special family tradition, at the very end of the Friday night meal:

Almonds and honey are sweets not to miss,
But none is as sweet as a Sabbath kiss.

. . . he saw a merchant with a large fish to sell.

Yosef
and the
Sabbath
Stone

LONG AGO, IN the mountains of Eritrea in East Africa, there lived a farmer named Yosef who had a small plot of land on a rocky hillside. In order to make ends meet, he would hire himself out as a laborer to Arha, a wealthy man who owned a neighboring farm. Every day, from sunup to sundown, Yosef would plow his neighbor's land, harvest the crops in their season, and bundle grain for market. Only in his spare time was he able to work his own small plot. He did this work for very little pay. The wealthy landowner kept all of the earnings from Yosef's labors to himself, keeping very strict accounts.

Despite these difficulties, Yosef remained steadfast in his work and never complained. If the landowner needed him to come at midnight because of a sudden storm, Yosef would come. If wild animals threatened the crops, Yosef would stand guard, waving them off. Through all this, Yosef's earnings remained small. But there was one thing that Yosef would never do, for he was devout in his observance of the Lord's commandments. Every week he would go to the *bet meqdas* — the house of worship — to hear the words of the Torah chanted by the *Qes* — the village priest. Once a year, with the rest of the community, he would climb the mountainside on *Sigd* — the holiest day of the year — to fast and pray. But of all sacred obligations, Yosef held most dear the commandment to honor the seventh day. He would not work on the Sabbath because, to Yosef, keeping the Sabbath was the most precious of all the traditions. It was on the Sabbath that Yosef felt that he was more than just a poor farmer struggling to eke a living from the soil. He was part of the Lord's work of creation, honored to carry out the sacred laws of the Torah.

So, every Friday in the early afternoon, he would put away Arha's plow and return to his modest home to prepare his house for the holy day. First, he swept all the dust and straw from the earthen floor. Then he would place kneaded dough into his brick oven to bake *dabo* — the round, flat

Sabbath bread. When all was ready, he put away his work-day vest and draped a white robe around his shoulders.

Arha kept to himself. He was lazy, but he didn't want to hire any help other than Yosef, knowing that nobody would work so hard for so little. In the hours that Yosef was away observing the Sabbath, the landowner would spend his time tallying his profits and counting his coins.

One afternoon as he sat under his olive tree going over his books and surveying his bushels of grain, the warmth of the sun and the gentle breezes lulled him to sleep. In his sleep, he had a dream. He found himself wandering on a hillside, when he heard a voice say, "Arha, everything that you possess will one day belong to your servant, Yosef. Be prepared to accept your fate." At this, Arha awoke with a start. "That was no dream," he said to himself. "That was a nightmare! I must do something to prevent it from coming true."

He thought about it for many days as he watched Yosef work in the fields. "This poor *falasha* will never be the master of my house!" Finally, Arha came up with a plan. The next week, while Yosef was away observing the Sabbath, Arha busily sold off everything that he owned, down to the last grain of wheat. Then he took the bags of coins and traveled to Addis Ababa, the capital city, to seek out a jewel merchant. Finally, he found what he was looking for: a ruby the size of a small peacock's egg, cut by the finest jeweler so that it reflected the light like a thousand red stars. He purchased the stone and placed it in a turban wrapped around his head.

On his way home he mused to himself, "Now my fortune is safe." Just as he approached his village, however, he crossed a narrow bridge over the river that cut through the mountain. At that same moment, a desert wind came whirling around him like an angry spirit. His clothes whipped at him, and he was nearly thrown from his donkey. The turban was ripped from his head. The glistening ruby was cast into the river by the roaring wind, and was carried away by the strong current. Arha was beside himself, but there was nothing he could do. Being unused to hard work, he never regained his fortune, but spent the rest of his days searching the wadis and riverbanks for his lost treasure.

Because he no longer worked for Arha, Yosef had to rely on his own small plot of land for his daily bread, but still he was determined to honor the Sabbath just as he had always done. One Friday afternoon he gathered up what coins he had and went to the marketplace. There, among the stalls, he saw a merchant with a large fish to sell. Yosef looked into his pockets and found that he had just enough money to buy it for Sabbath dinner. The merchant was glad to find a customer who would pay such a high price, and walked off with Yosef's coins jingling in his pocket.

Yosef hurried home. He wanted to make sure that

everything was ready by sundown. He found his sharpest knife and, placing the fish on a stone, he slit it open to clean it and remove the bones. All of a sudden, his knife struck something hard in the fish's belly, harder than any bone. To his surprise, when he peered inside, he saw something gleaming — it was a ruby, shining with the light of a thousand stars. Yosef removed the gem and thanked God for the miraculous gift.

From that day on, Yosef never had to struggle for his daily bread because he always had enough for himself. He shared his good fortune with his friends and neighbors, and was well known throughout the neighboring villages for his kindness and generosity. And every Friday afternoon, he swept his earthen floor, baked bread, and invited guests from far and near to share his Sabbath meal.

She felt a soft touch to her forehead . . .

Leah's Journey

ONCE IN ISRAEL, a young girl named Leah lived on a farm set back on a hillside overlooking the plains of the Galil. She had dark eyes and long dark hair that she wore in braids down her back. Every day it was her job to feed the chickens, give the cow its hay and, most important, to take the goats out to the nearby meadow to graze.

In the evenings after all of the work was done, the family gathered, and Leah's father told stories from the Torah. Leah would listen to the stories that their people had been telling one another for thousands of years. Most of all, she loved to hear the one of how, when Moses was a shepherd, he followed a lost lamb and came upon the burning bush, which told him of his people's destiny.

On Friday evenings, Leah's mother would light the Sabbath candles and sing a song of welcome to the Sabbath Queen. In the glowing candlelight, Leah would ask her mother if the Sabbath Queen was real or just a story. Her mother always gave her child the same answer, "No story is ever 'just a story.' In time you will see."

Sometimes, when Leah was in the meadow, she would wonder if she would ever witness a miracle like Moses had. But she knew that more important than miracles was tending to her work — the goats' milk, after all, helped to feed her family. One afternoon, while lost in these musings, one of the young goats wandered off. Leah looked everywhere, but couldn't find her in any of the usual grazing spots. "I can't go home without our goat," she thought, so she set out to find her. At first, she followed the familiar trails through the meadow, and the woods near her house, but still she saw no sign of the young goat. Leah went onward, following what she took to be the animal's tracks. As dusk approached, she found herself farther from home than she had ever been, in a strange part of the hills. Branches grew thickly overhead, blocking out the dying sunlight. The wind blew hard and drops of rain began to fall. A storm was blowing in from the sea.

Leah felt like giving up, but just then she heard a faint bleating. Following the sound, she came upon the entrance to a cave, hidden among the overhanging branches and leaves. Cautiously she entered and, there at the mouth of the cave, was the goat. Around the goat's neck was a shining golden rope, tethered to a stone. Leah wondered where the rope had come from. There was certainly nothing like it on their little farm. The goat stood there contentedly, nibbling on the stalks of grass at her hooves.

Leah saw that outside all was growing dark. The wind blew harder, and now sheets of rain began to fall. She wanted to take her little goat, turn around, and go home, but the darkness and rain blotted out the path. "How will I find my way?" she thought. Suddenly, far inside the cave, she saw a small flicker of light. Leaving the goat where it was tied, she followed the light into the cave, along a twisting path. The walls of the cave were damp and cold, but Leah kept her eyes on the flickering flame and moved ahead. Finally, she emerged from the dark tunnel into a room whose like she had never seen before. Its walls were of polished stone, and the ceiling was lined with cedar beams that filled the room with their scent. In the middle of the room was a grand table with shining silver and gem-studded glasses, as if a banquet was about to begin. The light that she had seen came from two candles, and standing near them was a regal-looking woman. Her hair was crowned with flowers, and her dress was of shimmering white, trimmed with silver and blue thread. She looked up and smiled at her visitor.

"Welcome to my home," the woman said. "I was just about to say the blessing over the candles." She offered Leah a basin of water to wash her hands.

Leah drew near to the table and watched as the beautiful woman sang the blessings, circling her arms, as if bringing the light into the room. Leah found herself joining in with a whisper of "Amen," as her hostess said blessings over a cup of wine, and two loaves of braided bread. "You must be hungry after searching so long. Come, join me for a meal."

They spent the rest of the evening singing at the table. Carried away by the beauty of the woman's voice, Leah found herself singing words and melodies that she had never heard before.

Later that night, as she drifted off to sleep on a luxurious bed of silken pillows, Leah murmured, "Who are you?"

"You sing about me every Friday night. I am the Sabbath Queen, and now you are in my home. Rest well."

When Leah awoke, she looked around, wondering if all that had happened the night before was a dream. But no, she was in the same beautiful room. Around the table, several new guests were gathered. Although Leah had never seen any of them before, she recognized all of their names as the Sabbath Queen introduced each one. Abraham sat with his wife, Sarah, and across the table sat Moses with Aaron, his brother, and their sister Miriam.

Leah sat in awe as she listened to them studying the words of the Torah together all morning long. As the guests left, the Sabbath Queen invited Leah to stay for the whole day. Late in the afternoon, she offered her a plate of dates and almonds for the last meal of the Sabbath day. Once again, she sang the sweetest of melodies in her silvery voice.

Finally, she told Leah, "Our time together is almost at an end. Go outside the cave and watch the sky for the first three stars that you can see." Leah did as she was told, returning to the cave after the sky was lit by three stars. Inside the hall, the Sabbath Queen stood over the table, now set with a jeweled box of sweet-smelling spices, a goblet of wine, and a candle twisted from many different tapers. "It is time for us to separate. Smell these spices, so that you may remember our time together. Hold your hands up to the light of this candle, and keep its glow in your heart. Now hold the candle and, as I say this last blessing, extinguish the flames in the wine." Leah did as she was told. As she dipped the candle in the wine, the cave instantly became dark, but Leah was not afraid, because she could hear the Queen's voice telling her that Elijah — the Prophet himself — would lead her from the cave. She heard faint footsteps, leading her onward as she made her way down the mountain paths.

Leah returned to her farm just as her mother was calling her in to light the Shabbat candles. She felt a soft touch on her forehead and heard a voice that whispered,

"Shalom, Leah. Your journey is over." Looking down, Leah saw the goat standing beside her, the golden tether still tied loosely around its neck. Leah led the creature, who was bleating softly, back to the flock, and then entered her home. It was as if she had never been gone — and yet, how far she had come!

As her mother lit the candles and sang the song of welcome, Leah listened to her own thoughts. She knew that while she might never again find herself in the Sabbath Queen's magical realm, her family would always invite this wondrous guest to their home in the hills of the Galil. And the memory of each Shabbat, with its glowing candles, soft melodies, and sweet spices, would stay with each of them through all the days of the week — until the Sabbath Queen arrived again.

Glossary
and
Pronunciation
Guide

HERE ARE THE PRONUNCIATIONS FOR NAMES AND WORDS IN THE
STORIES. THE SOUND *"ch"* IN HEBREW OR YIDDISH SOUNDS LIKE
THE ENDING OF THE COMPOSER'S NAME BA*ch*.

ARHA (AR-hah) A common Ethiopian name, as cited by Harold
Courlander in his book *The Fire on the Mountain: Tales from Ethiopia
and Eritrea.*

BETA ISRAEL (BAY-tah YIS-rah-el) The name meaning
"House of Israel," which the Jewish communities of Ethiopia and
Eritrea called themselves throughout their history. According to

scholarly sources, the Beta Israel was established in Ethiopia from the time of the destruction of the First Temple in 586 BCE.

BET MEQDAS (bayt MEK-dahs) The central house of worship, similar to a synagogue, for the communities of Beta Israel in Ethiopia.

BRACHA (BRACH-chah) The Hebrew word for "blessing" comes from a word meaning "to bend over" or "kneel." Blessings in the Jewish tradition have particular forms, depending on the ceremony or specific situation.

CHALLAH (CHAH-lah) A traditional type of bread, often braided, which is eaten on the Sabbath and other holidays. On the Sabbath, it is customary for two loaves to be placed on the table as a symbol of God's bounty.

DABO (DAH-bo) The name for the round, flat bread that Ethiopian Jews bake for the Sabbath evening meal.

DIASPORA (dye-AS-poh-rah) The word Diaspora — in Hebrew, "Galut" (gah-LOOT) — means exile. Historically, the exile dates from the first century CE, when Rome destroyed the Second Temple and drove the Jewish people from Jerusalem and their homeland in ancient Judea. Even today, Jews who do not live in Israel are still considered to be part of the Diaspora.

DON ISAACO (dawn ee-SAH-koh) The Ladino or Judeo-Spanish pronunciation of the name "Isaac." Although our story's Don Isaaco is fictitious, Don Isaac Abrabanel (1437–1540 CE) was a famous Biblical scholar and financier whose noble family lived in Seville, Spain for many generations.

ERITREA (eh-REE-tree-uh) A country to the northwest of Ethiopia, in eastern Africa, that borders on the Red Sea, which was home to communities of Beta Israel until Operation Moses — mass airlifts to Israel — took place in 1984, when many Ethiopian Jews were forced to flee their country due to civil war and discrimination.

FALASHA (fah-LAH-shah) The Amharic (Ethiopian language) word for "stranger." This is a derogatory term applied to the members of Beta Israel, the Jewish community of Ethiopia and Eritrea, which lived there for many centuries.

GALIL (gah-LEEL) The Hebrew word for Galilee, the northern region of Israel, which is referred to in the biblical books of Joshua and Chronicles, as well as the Talmud and New Testament.

HALACHAH (hah-lah-CHAH) Literally, "the way." This is the Hebrew word for Jewish laws, from both oral and written traditions, which have guided the Jewish people for many centuries.

HAVDALAH (hahv-DAH-lah) Literally, "separation." This is the name for the ceremony that ends the Sabbath and begins the new week. The ritual includes blessings over wine, the smelling of fragrant spices, and the lighting of a special braided candle.

L'CHAH DODI (leh-CHAH doh-DEE) Literally means "Come my beloved." These are the first words of a song dating back to the sixteenth century, which welcomes the Sabbath as a bride.

KABBALISTIC (kah-bah-LISS-tik) Refers to the Kabbalah, the most commonly used term for the mystical teachings of the Jewish tradition, whose scholars produced important texts such as *The Zohar* (*The Book of Splendor*), especially in the Middle Ages from the twelfth century onward.

KIDDUSH (KIH-dush) This is the Yiddish pronunciation of a Hebrew word for a special blessing said at Shabbat and other holidays, in which God is thanked and remembered for taking the Jewish people out of slavery in Egypt and for giving them the Torah.

MELACHOT (meh-lah-CHOTE) In Hebrew, the plural form of melacha — any one of thirty-nine activities associated with human productivity or skills which are prohibited on the Sabbath. These are enumerated in *The Mishnah,* a central book of Jewish law based on oral teachings, which was codified in the second century CE.

MIDRASH (MID-rahsh) This term comes from the Hebrew word that means "to explain, to draw out." A midrash is a rabbinic tale or legend that is used to explain or embellish verses of the Torah.

MOTTKE (MOT-keh) This is a Yiddish name for a boy, based on the Hebrew name Mordecai. "Mottkele," (MOT-keh-leh) is a version used as a term of endearment.

ONEG SHABBAT (OH-neg shah-BAHT) Literally, "Sabbath delight" is the tradition of singing songs and telling stories after the Friday night meal to continue the joy of welcoming the Sabbath into the home.

PHILISTINE (FILL-ih-steen) A people of Aegean origin occupying the south coast of ancient Palestine — called Philistia in the Bible — who were often at war with the Israelites.

QES (KESS) Among the Beta Israel, the Qes is the holy man who is responsible for knowledge of ritual, prayer, and sacred writings in the community.

SAFED (SAH-fed) A principal town in the north of Israel, situated on a mountain north of Tiberias. A Jewish community has been in existence in Safed since at least the first century CE. In the sixteenth century, an important group of Jewish scholars and mystics lived and taught in Safed.

SEUDAH SHLISHIT (seh-oo-DAH shlee-SHEET) Literally, "third meal." Seuda shlishit is eaten after Saturday evening prayers. It is the last meal of the Sabbath before havdalah.

SHABBAT MENUCHAH (shah-BAHT meh-new-CHAH) Literally, "menuchah" means rest. There are many different ways of describing the Sabbath in the Jewish tradition. This name refers to the break from weekday activity that the Sabbath grants.

SHAVUA TOV (shah-VOO-ah TOVE) Literally, "good week." An expression for the end of the Sabbath, it is a wish for health and prosperity in the coming days until the next Friday evening.

SIGD (SEE-gid) The most important holy day for the communities of Beta Israel. On the morning of Sigd, the Beta Israel carry their Torah to the top of a mountain, where they fast and pray. At midday, they come down from the mountain and hold a communal feast and celebration.

VITEBSK (vee-TEBSK) The capital city of the Vitebsk region of Byelorussia (a province of the former Soviet Socialist Republic) where a Jewish community was established at the end of the sixteenth century. At various times, Vitebsk was annexed to Lithuania, Poland, and Russia, due to wars and territorial conflicts.

YOM KIPPUR (YOHM kee-POOR) Literally, the day of atonement. This is considered to be the holiest day of the Jewish calendar, on which Jews fast and pray for forgiveness for their sins from God and their fellows. In Midrashic, or rabbinic oral tradition, Yom Kippur was also thought to exist before the creation of the world.

ZEMER (ZEH-mer) From the Hebrew word for "song." *Zemirot* (zeh-meer-OTE in plural form) are table hymns sung during or directly after the Sabbath meal. The custom of singing zemirot is found today in Israel and throughout the Diaspora.

About
the
Stories

1. THE MOST IMPORTANT DAY

This is a tale woven around the images of creation from the book of
Genesis. I first read this story in a Hebrew study text, as passed on to
me in 1992 by my mother, Grace Jaffe, and by Vivian Finkel, the
Hebrew language teacher at Park Avenue Synagogue in New York
City.

2. SABBATH SPICE

The original source for this story dates back to the early Talmudic
era, about 200 CE. In that version, it is attributed to Rabbi Joshua
ben Hananiah — a scholar who lived in ancient Israel during the

reign of the Roman empire in the second century CE. In this collection, the story is set during the sixth century BCE after the destruction of the First Temple, when many Jews had to leave their homes and cities to settle in the empires of Babylonia, Egypt, and Persia. Although not originally a character in the story, the Emperor Cyrus, who ruled Persia from 559–529 BCE, was historically known for his tolerance and acceptance of the exiled Jewish community. Several ancient Jewish texts, including the Book of Ezra and the Book of Daniel, as well as the biblical books of Isaiah and Psalms, cite his name and deeds in prophetic verses. Nehemiah is the name of a Jewish noble who attained royal favor during the reign of Artaxerxes I (465–425 BCE).

3.   KING DAVID AND THE SPIDER

This a story that is known in many sources in Jewish legend. King Saul's rages and jealousy of David are written about explicitly in the Bible (First Samuel, verses XIV; XVIII). King David was also known as a musician and composer, as well as a formidable military leader. Many of his songs are recorded in the book of Psalms and have become part of the Sabbath liturgy. This story is one of the many legends that grew up around the name and memory of this revered king of Israel. Earlier versions can be found in Louis Ginzberg's *Legends of the Jews,* and in Ellen Frankel's collection *The Classic Tales: 4,000 Years of Jewish Folklore.*

4.   MOTTKE'S CHICKEN

This story can be found in *A Treasury of Jewish Folklore* by Nathan Ausubel, under the title "Why Waste a Ruble?" The narrative motif of the fool or simpleton who continues to exchange one thing for another exists in international folklore as well, in such tales as "Lazy

Jack" (England) and "Simple Hans" (Germany). Mottke is a character who may be related to the character of Mottke Chabad, known in Yiddish folklore for his trickery as well as his foolish ways.

5. A RIDDLE AND A KISS

This story is a retelling of a "romance," a folktale from the Sephardic or Judeo-Spanish tradition, as cited in *Types and Motifs of the Judeo-Spanish Folktales,* by Reginatta Haboucha. This story is an example of an "oicotype," that is, a universal tale that has been transformed to fit a particular group's language and customs. The story is known in the folklore of Spain and was carried to other parts of the Spanish empire, such as Puerto Rico and Mexico. The elements of the teasing rhymes between the noble youth and the clever youngest daughter are common to all versions of this tale. However, it is only in the Sephardic Jewish version that the youngest daughter exchanges her kisses for a "Sabbath fish." For a version in the Spanish tradition, see "The Basil Plant" in the *Encyclopedia of Puerto Rico,* Vol. 12.

6. YOSEF AND THE SABBATH STONE

This story, most often known under the title of "Joseph, Who Loved the Sabbath," is based on a tale from the Babylonian Talmud that has found its way into many versions of rabbinic legend and the oral tradition. I have set the story among the Beta Israel, or Jews of Ethiopia, who are among the most recent immigrant groups to the state of Israel, as well as to North America and Canada. Fuller descriptions of Ethiopian Jewish tradition and customs can be found in *The Evolution of the Ethiopian Jews,* by James Quirin. Some of the ethnographic details in the story were provided by the exhibition *The Jews of Ethiopia: The Last Glimpse of a 3,000 Year Old Community* at the Eldridge Street Synagogue (New York City/July, 1998).

7. LEAH'S JOURNEY

This retelling is based on a theme to be found in several stories from Jewish oral tradition and literature from eastern Europe in which a pious person — usually a scholar or rabbi — is lost in the forest and finds his way (or is led) to the palace of a spiritual figure such as the Sabbath Queen or, in some cases, Elijah the Prophet. I first came across this story years ago in Israel, in a Hebrew collection of tales for young children. In S. Y. Agnon's tale, "The Fable of the Goat" (see Bibliography, Strassfeld), a rabbi's son, in search of his lost animal, is led to the Holy Land. In another version, in Hasidic lore (see Bibliography, Wiener), a young scholar trying to find his way home gets lost in a forest, and spends the Sabbath studying with the Prophet Elijah, who then leads him home.

Bibliography

AUSUBEL, NATHAN, ED. *A Treasury of Jewish Folklore.* New York: Crown Publishers, 1948, 1975.

BAEZ, VINCENTE, ED. *Encyclopedia of Puerto Rico* (Vol. 12). Madrid: Corredera, 1976.

BARACK, NATHAN A. *A History of the Sabbath.* New York: Jonathan David, 1965.

BIN GORION, MICHA JOSEPH, ED. *Mimekor Yisrael: Selected Classical Jewish Folktales.* Bloomington: Indiana University Press, 1990.

BUBER, MARTIN. *The Legend of the Baal-Shem.* New York: Harper & Row, 1995.

Tales of the Hasidim. New York: Schocken Books, 1947, 1997.

CERTNER, SIMON, ED. *101 Jewish Stories: A Treasury of*

Folktales from Midrash and Other Sources. New York: Board of Jewish Education of Greater New York, 1961, 1983.

COURLANDER, HAROLD, AND WOLF LESLAU. *The Fire on the Mountain and Other Tales from Ethiopia and Eritrea.* New York: Henry Holt and Co., 1950, 1995.

ELIZAR-EPSTEIN, RABBI. *Sabbath Chapters of Talmud.* Jerusalem: The Jewish Agency, 1972.

FRANKEL, ELLEN. *The Classic Tales: 4,000 Years of Jewish Lore.* Northvale, New Jersey: Jason Aronson, Inc., 1989.

GARTENBERG, LEO, ED. *Israel Legends.* Tel Aviv, Israel: Machborot L'Sifrut Publishers, 1969.

GINSBERG, ELIOTT. *Sod Ha-Shabbat: The Mystery of the Sabbath.* New York: State University of New York Press, 1989.

GINZBERG, LOUIS. *The Legends of the Jews.* Philadelphia: The Jewish Publication Society, 1934.

GRODENWITZ, PETER. *The Music of Israel from the Biblical to the Modern Era.* Portland, Oregon: Amadeus Press, 1996.

GRUNFELD, ISIDOR. *The Sabbath: A Guide to Its Understanding and Observance.* New York: Philip Feldheim, 1959.

HABOUCHA, REGINATTA. *Types and Motifs of the Judeo-Spanish Folktales.* New York: Garland Publishing, 1992.

HESCHEL, ABRAHAM JOSHUA. *The Sabbath: Its Meaning for Modern Man.* New York: Farrar, Straus, and Young, 1951.

The Holy Scriptures According to the Masoretic Text. Philadelphia: The Jewish Publication Society, 1955.

ISAACS, RONALD H. *Shabbat Delight.* New York: Ktav Publishing House, 1986.

LANDMAN, ISRAEL, ED. *The Universal Jewish Encyclopedia: An Authoritative and Popular Presentation of Jews and Judaism Since Earliest Times.* (Vol. 8, 9). New York: Ktav Publishing House, 1942, 1969.

LAREDO, VICTOR. *Sephardic Spain.* New York: Editorial Mensaje, 1978.

MILLGRAM, ABRAHAM. *Sabbath: The Day of Delight.* Philadelphia: The Jewish Publication Society, 1944.

PATAI, JOSEPH. *Souls and Secrets: Hasidic Stories.* Northvale, New Jersey: Jason Aronson, Inc., 1995.

QUIRIN, JAMES. *The Evolution of the Ethiopian Jews.* Philadelphia: University of Pennsylvania Press, 1992.

ROTH, CECIL, ED. *Encyclopedia Judaica.* Jerusalem: Keter Publishing House, 1972.

ROTH, JOAN. Unpublished exhibition materials from *The Jews of Ethiopia: The Last Glimpse of a 3,000 Year Old Community.* Eldridge Street Synagogue, New York City, July, 1998.

SCHOLEM, GERSHOM, ED. *Zohar/The Book of Splendor: Basic Readings from the Kabbalah.* New York: Schocken Books, 1949, 1963.

STRASSFELD, MICHAEL. *A Shabbat Haggadah.* New York: The American Jewish Committee, 1981.

WIENER, AHARON. *The Prophet Elijah in the Development of Judaism: A Depth-Psychological Study.* London: Routledge and Kegan Paul, 1978.

WIESEL, ELIE. *Souls on Fire: Portraits and Legends of Hasidic Masters.* New York: Random House, 1972.

Recommended
Reading

BIALIK, HAYIM NAHMAN, AND YEHOSHUA HANA RAVNITZKY, EDS. *The Book of Legends: Sefer ha Aggadah; Legends from the Talmud and Midrash.* New York: Schocken Books, 1992.

GOLDIN, BARBARA DIAMOND. *A Child's Book of Midrash: 52 Stories from the Jewish Sages.* Northvale, New Jersey: Jason Aronson, Inc., 1990.

GREENBERG, RABBI SIDNEY. *A Treasury of Sabbath Inspiration.* New York: United Synagogue of Conservative Judaism, 1995.

HIRSCH, MARILYN. *Joseph, Who Loved the Sabbath.* New York: Viking Kestrel, 1986.

HOLTZ, BARRY W., ED. *Back to the Sources: Reading the Classic Jewish Texts.* New York: Summit Books, 1984.

JAFFE, NINA. *The Uninvited Guest and Other Jewish Holiday Tales.* New York: Scholastic, 1993.

SCHWARTZ, HOWARD. *The Sabbath Lion: A Jewish Folktale from Algeria.* New York: HarperCollins, 1992.

SCHRAMM, PENINNAH. *Chosen Tales: Stories Told by Jewish Storytellers.* Northvale, New Jersey: Jason Aronson Inc., 1995.

ZEITLIN, STEVE. *Because God Loves Stories: An Anthology of Jewish Storytelling.* New York: Simon & Schuster, 1997.

About
the
Author

NINA JAFFE IS the respected author of, most recently, *The Mysterious Visitor: Stories of the Prophet Elijah*, and *The Uninvited Guest and Other Jewish Holiday Tales* which won the 1993 Sydney Taylor Award and was an American Bookseller "Pick of the Lists." Some of her other books are *Patakín: World Tales of Drums and Drummers*; *In the Month of Kislev: A Story for Hanukkah*; and *The Golden Flower: A Tainto Myth from Puerto Rico*. She is on the graduate faculty at Bank Street College of Education as a specialist in storytelling, folklore, and music. Ms. Jaffe lives in New York City with her husband and son.

Other Scholastic Press Titles by Nina Jaffe

The Mysterious Visitor: Stories of the Prophet Elijah

Illustrated by Elivia Savadier

The Uninvited Guest and Other Jewish Holiday Tales

Illustrated by Elivia Savadier